What Grandma Built

Michelle Gilman

illustrated by Jazmin Sasky

 HARBOUR PUBLISHING

HARBOUR PUBLISHING CO. LTD.
PO Box 219, Madeira Park, BC, V0N 2H0
www.harbourpublishing.com

Illustrations by Jazmin Sasky, www.jazminsasky.com
Copyedited by Shirarose Wilensky
Cover and text design by Shed Simas
Printed and bound in Canada
Printed on paper certified by the Forest Stewardship Council

Harbour Publishing acknowledges the support of the Canada Council
for the Arts, which last year invested $157 million to bring the arts to
Canadians throughout the country. We also gratefully acknowledge
financial support from the Government of Canada through the Canada
Book Fund and from the Province of British Columbia through the
BC Arts Council and the Book Publishing Tax Credit.

**CATALOGUING DATA AVAILABLE FROM
LIBRARY AND ARCHIVES CANADA**
ISBN 978-1-55017-753-4 (paper)
ISBN 978-1-55017-754-1 (ebook)

Mom, we promise to continue your legacy and keep building your castle, with all the love and devotion we have in our hearts. And, indeed, it will be "grand."

We love you now and always.
—Michelle Gilman

Did you know my grandma built a castle?

Let me tell you how she did it...

When she was young, Grandma fell in love with Grandpa, and they began building a life together.

First, they decided to build a house. They could not have known it would end up being so much more than just an ordinary house. To my family, it was a magical place.

Grandma and Grandpa searched and searched for just the right spot.

They found a beautiful piece of land right beside a lake. Grandma loved the smell of the grassy field, the view of the lake and the sound of the loons.

Grandma wanted a home they could live in for years and years, so they built their house on a stone foundation that would be strong enough to last forever.

Grandma and Grandpa had two daughters and a son. Grandma loved playing, singing and laughing with her children.

She was the kind of mom who had a way of making ordinary days seem extraordinary.

And when things went wrong, Grandma was always there to offer advice or a hug.

Grandma and Grandpa's children grew up fast. Before long, they were getting married and starting families of their own.

Grandma wanted her house to have enough room for everyone in the growing family. So she added extra bedrooms, bunk beds and lots of toys.

On the grassy field, Grandma put in a giant playground. She had so much fun swinging, sliding and climbing with her grandchildren.

Grandma and Grandpa built a big dining room overlooking the lake. Everyone looked forward to lively discussions over Grandma's homemade dinners.

Each of us had an important job: watering the flowers, feeding the hummingbirds or helping in the kitchen. With the family's help, Grandma filled every room with warmth and love.

Grandma lined her walls with family pictures and her grandchildren's drawings. She reserved one incredible wall just to measure the kids' growth from year to year.

One summer, Grandma and Grandpa started a garden.
They planted flowers, berries and herbs.

Grandma would pick ripe, juicy berries and fruit and bake
the most delicious pies: apple-raspberry, blueberry and
everyone's favourite, strawberry-rhubarb.

Every day, Grandma would walk down to the lake with us. Along the way, we'd pick wildflowers and look at birds.

In the middle of the lake was a little island where the seagulls lived. Grandma named it "Seagull Island" and always packed seeds to feed the birds.

Of course, the loons were Grandma's favourite.

At the end of each fun day, the grandchildren watched movies in Grandma and Grandpa's big cozy bed, while Grandma talked with her children over tea.

One day, Grandma wasn't feeling well. Everyone cared for her with so much love. But as the weeks passed, Grandma wasn't getting better.

Sadly, no one lives forever—not even Grandma.

After Grandma died, the family gathered around her dining-room table to share stories and memories. That's when we realized exactly what she had created.

Grandma created so much more than an ordinary house. It was full of love and traditions. She created "Grandma's Castle," a special and magical place. And it *was* built to last forever—especially in the hearts and memories of our family.

Grandma's work is done. Now, it's our turn to continue her traditions.

Do you know what that means?

Side by side,
year after year...

using Grandma's everlasting love as
our guide, we will continue building
Grandma's Castle together.

What Grandma Built *is a
tribute to Phyllis Shenkarow.*

*Grandma's Castle is located in Lake of the Woods, Ontario.
It has been growing along with our family for more than
twenty years. It is, indeed, a magical place.*